Rolf and Edgar

By Rosalyn Rosenbluth

Illustrated by Ernest Socolov

GREEN TIGER PRESS, INC.

Text copyright © 1990 by Rosalyn Rosenbluth
Illustrations copyright © 1990 by Ernest Socolov
Green Tiger Press, 435 East Carmel Street
  San Marcos, California 92069-4362
ISBN 0-88138-140-3
First Edition
10 9 8 7 6 5 4 3 2 1

Manufactured in Hong Kong

For Jack, who believes in me —R.R.
To Marc Benjamin with all my love —E.S.

In a dark forest, near a high mountain, lived two trolls—Rolf and Edgar. They wore pointed hats and baggy pants. They lived in a little hut. They were just like all the other trolls in the forest, except for one thing. Rolf never looked up and Edgar never looked down.

Every day Rolf and Edgar hiked from their hut to the high mountain. On the way Edgar watched clouds and birds. Rolf peered at ants and mushrooms.

"Look here," Edgar said. "There are ripe apples on this tree. Let's pick some to eat later."

But Rolf would not look up. "I am picking mushrooms," he muttered. "I do not want apples."

Sometimes Rolf called out, "Look at this mole, Edgar."

But Edgar would not look down. "I am watching eagles," he said. "Why would I want to look at moles?"

Often Edgar tripped and fell into holes as he walked. Then Rolf laughed. "If you looked down, you would never fall into holes."

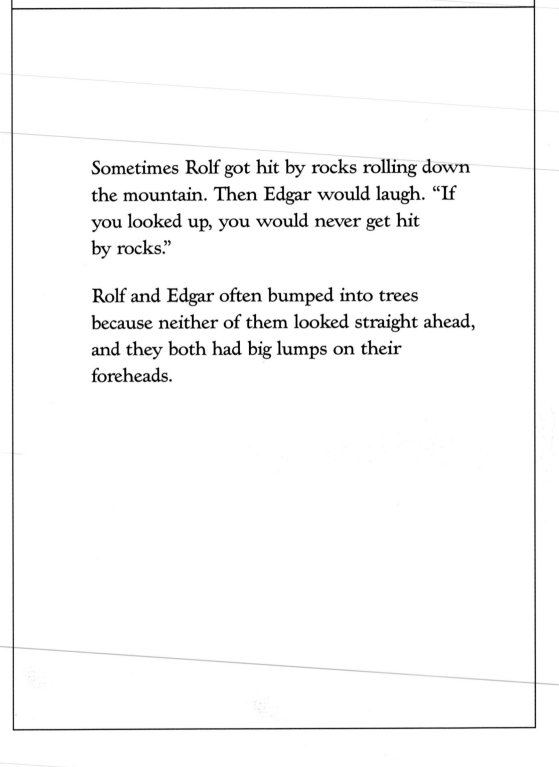

Sometimes Rolf got hit by rocks rolling down
the mountain. Then Edgar would laugh. "If
you looked up, you would never get hit
by rocks."

Rolf and Edgar often bumped into trees
because neither of them looked straight ahead,
and they both had big lumps on their
foreheads.

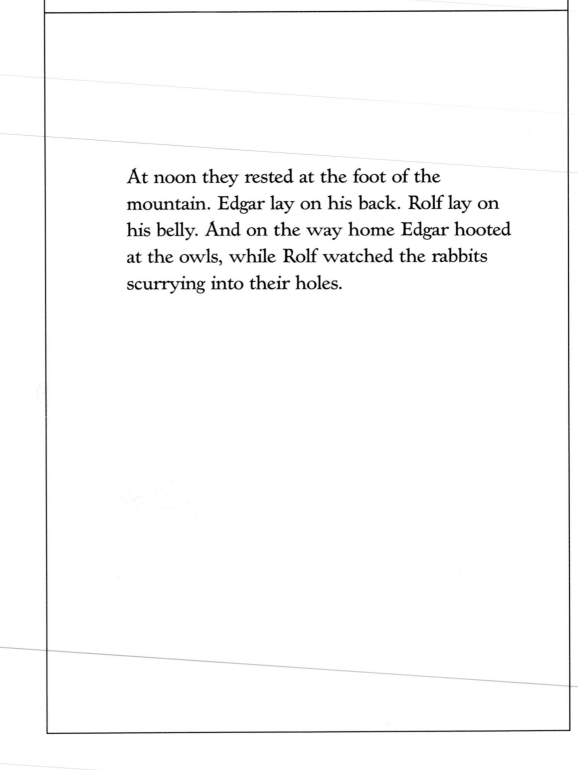

At noon they rested at the foot of the mountain. Edgar lay on his back. Rolf lay on his belly. And on the way home Edgar hooted at the owls, while Rolf watched the rabbits scurrying into their holes.

One morning the trolls set out on their usual walk. "The bluebells are out," cried Rolf happily. "Spring is here."

"I saw a robin fly by last week," said Edgar. "I knew spring was here even then."

When they came to the mountain the little trolls lay down to rest. But Edgar changed his mind. "I think I will go see if the robin's eggs have hatched."

"Go ahead," said Rolf. "I will watch these ants for a while."

Edgar went into the forest. It was easy for him to climb because he was looking up. But when he got to the nest he saw that the eggs had not hatched. "Humph," said Edgar. He started to climb down, but this was not so easy. He had to feel for the branches with his toes. At last he reached the ground and walked back to the mountain.

"The eggs have not hatched yet," he said. But no one answered. "The eggs have not hatched yet," he called loudly. But all he heard was the wind.

This had never happened before. Edgar smiled at a butterfly that flew past his face. Then he studied the sky for a while. Finally he cupped his hands to his mouth. "Can you hear me, Rolf?" he yelled. But Rolf did not answer.

"Maybe he has gone into the forest," thought Edgar. He walked back along the path calling Rolf's name. He yelled and shouted. But no one answered.

Edgar went back to the mountain. He was very alarmed. What had happened to Rolf? He did not see anything in the sky to tell him what had happened. He did not see anything in the trees to tell him what had happened.

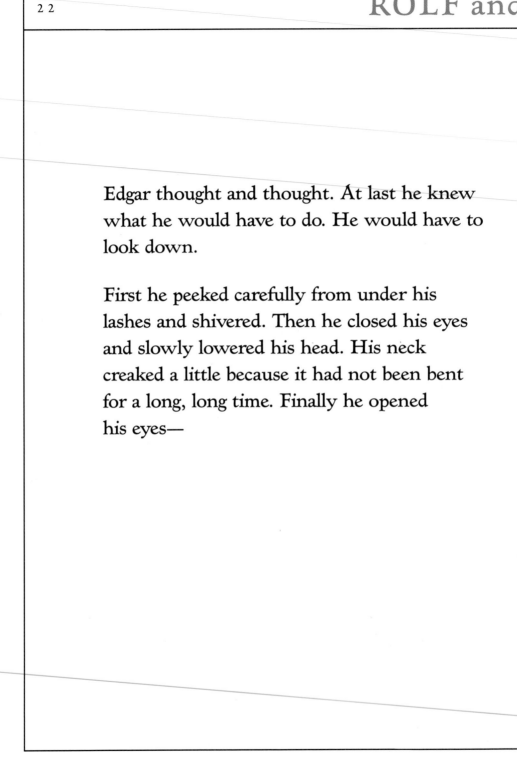

Edgar thought and thought. At last he knew what he would have to do. He would have to look down.

First he peeked carefully from under his lashes and shivered. Then he closed his eyes and slowly lowered his head. His neck creaked a little because it had not been bent for a long, long time. Finally he opened his eyes—

There at his feet lay Rolf. He was on his back and his eyes were closed. His round cheeks were pale. A big rock lay next to him.

Edgar fell to his knees. "Rolf, Rolf," he cried. "If only I had looked down before, I would have seen you."

Edgar rubbed Rolf's hands. He patted his cheeks. At last Rolf opened his eyes. The first thing he saw was a cloud. "What is that pretty thing?" he asked.

"It's a cloud, Rolf," Edgar shouted happily.

"Is that what the top of the mountain looks like!" Rolf exclaimed. "If I had looked up, I would have seen that rock before it hit me."

"And here are the ants you were watching!" Edgar cried. "Is this a bluebell?"

That night Edgar saw rabbits for the first time. Rolf watched the moon in wonder.

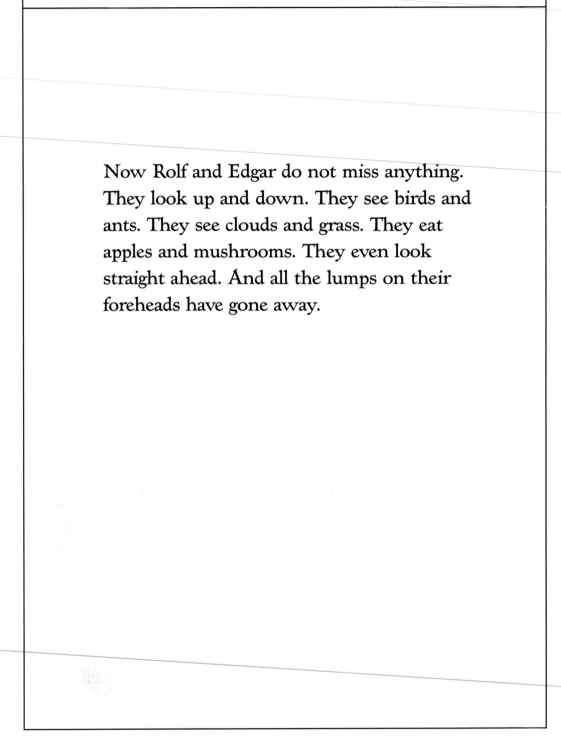

Now Rolf and Edgar do not miss anything. They look up and down. They see birds and ants. They see clouds and grass. They eat apples and mushrooms. They even look straight ahead. And all the lumps on their foreheads have gone away.